Writing in Virginia's Shadow

Also by Mary Pomfret and published by Ginninderra Press
Cleaning Out the Closet

Mary Pomfret

Writing in Virginia's Shadow

Acknowledgements

I thank Dr Sue Gillett of La Trobe University Bendigo campus, for her professional support, encouragement and friendship in the writing of these stories.

Members of Scribblers listened patiently to the words on these pages and I thank them for their guidance and generosity. I especially want to thank my fellow students at La Trobe University and lecturers Dr Sophia Ahlberg and Dr Rodney Blackhirst, as well as Bendigo Regional Institute of TAFE Professional Writing and Editing course coordinator Dr Ian Irvine and former teacher, John Holton.

I must acknowledge all my soul sisters – the beautiful women in my life from whom I have learnt so much. I am eternally grateful to my sister Tess, who has listened to me endlessly. Without you all, I would never have made it through

Finally, I would like to thank both my beautiful son, Eric, who is the subject of my poem 'Child Portrait' and my husband and friend, John, for many things but, above all else, for their enduring love.

An early version of 'Homage to Eveline' appeared in *Hecate* in 2010 under the pen name Mia Francis. 'Heart Jottings' contains excerpts from previously published works as follows: 'Missing' in *Tamba*, 'Love Jacket New England Review Tristesse' in *Hecate*, 'Venus' in *Idiom* 23, 'Mother Superior's Garden Party' in *Idiom* 23 and *Irish Heritage Journal*, 'Child Portrait' in *Painted Words*, 'Our Darker Purpose' in *Thirst*, 'Joe, 1971' in *Culture Is…*, and 'Peripheral Vision' in *Idiom* 23 and *Scintillea*.

GINNINDERRA PRESS
PO Box 3461 Port Adelaide 5015
www.ginninderrapress.com.au

For my mother Eileen, who always found a way

'...a woman must have money
and a room of her own if she is
to write fiction...'

Virginia Woolf, 1929

our little magazine
PO Box 1
Somewhere in a Capital City
Australia

Dear Margot

Thank you for your recent submission to our magazine. We read your trilogy *Writing in Virginia's Shadow* with interest, and although your work is stylistically unsuited to our publication, we are happy to provide you with feedback.

We feel that your piece is far too long for an Australian literary journal, and we suggest that you submit these stories separately as single stories. We struggle to see your reason for connecting the stories, and even if it is an attempt at post-modern structure, it doesn't work. The devices you use to connect the stories, such as recurring metaphors, motifs, related characters and the repeated theme of the 'poor woebegone struggling women writer', are tedious, pretentious and far from subtle.

We feel that you are labouring a point which has been done to death. You are beating the poor unsuspecting reader about the head with an outdated theme. A single story with this theme may just pass with an editor, but three interrelated stories with this old boring chestnut – no.

The most troubling aspect of your stories, we feel, is the lack of redemption for the female characters. You leave them all stuck in the quicksand of their own hopeless neediness, dependency, passivity and repression. We feel we want to scream at all these characters, 'Get a life!' but of course we wouldn't; we are far too polite. Furthermore, we find the floating disembodied character, Margot, your namesake, who is seemingly the fictitious author of all the stories, intolerable. Eliminate her.

We wish you luck with your writing and encourage you to submit again.

Sincerely yours,
Davida, Francis & Robbie

Showing up

Albino writers are about as unusual as albino policemen – the albino condition being, on the whole, a rarity. In all his thirty-three years, Sam never made an issue of his albinism but, if he could, he used it to his advantage. Tonight he felt at ease in his priest's garb and dog collar, the starkness of the black frock contrasting with his ash-blond hair. The robe covered his gut that hung over the waist of his jeans and, with just a bit of his sister's kohl pencil around his eyes, he thought he looked dramatic. Nigel had said that a bit of theatre at a book launch was a good thing.

Infinity and Beyond wasn't a hardback. Nigel had advised against it for a first novel. He'd recommended The Church as a venue for the launch. And he was right. It had class and ambience. Nigel had said to be sure to have glasses and not disposable cups for the wine and he'd suggested plenty of cabinet sauvignon, a few good chardonnays, and casks for when the bottles ran dry. He said it was very important to start with bottles because, after a few, people didn't know what they were drinking and it was easy to switch to casks once cheeks started to glow. Have plenty of booze and you'll sell plenty of books, Nigel said.

A strong smell of sandalwood oil wafted through the hall as Nigel walked in. He was wearing a black polo neck jumper, his long brown locks tied back tightly in a ponytail. Sam always thought of Nigel as having that certain quintessential coolness that made him stand out from the crowd. He always looked slightly shabby, just enough to give the impression of being artistic and unconcerned but never, never scruffy. Being tall and athletically built probably helped Nigel's charisma and Sam was aware of at least one student who had a raging crush on him.

Sam had often thought what he would do if he had only half of Nigel's ability to pull the chicks. Man, what he wouldn't do? The writing thing helped get the girls in, though. They liked that kind of thing. Sam tried to copy Nigel's easy manner with women. Probably needed more practice, though.

Nigel Langhorn had been Sam's creative writing tutor in his first undergraduate year and Sam had asked him to write the blurb.

> *Infinity and Beyond* is a dazzling first novel, richly textured and intellectually challenging. A post-modern work of extraordinary intelligence demonstrating mimetic emotion, crackling with energy and resonating with anger and vision.
>
> Nigel Langhorne, author of *The Emperor's Dream*

Sam was pleased with that. Nigel understood him, and his work.

'You look great, man,' said Nigel, shaking Sam's hand. 'Just as long as the old darlings know that you're here to sell books not to hear confession!' Nigel poured himself a large red from one of the opened bottles lined up on the bar. 'Try and keep the conversation brief, though, because too much chatter during the signing holds up the book sales, and that's what we're here for my old son, isn't it?' Nigel slapped Sam on the shoulder.

The novel was displayed in high stacks on an old timber desk.

People began to arrive: women in tweed skirts and woolly hats, grey-haired bearded men in corduroy pants, scarlet-haired ageing hippy females and a few frowning children. A fairly typical crew, thought Nigel. Nearly half of the bottled wine was already gone. This lot were really quaffing it down. All the better for sales, Nigel thought. It had been a bit of a strain financing Sam for this book, but once it started selling he would double his investment. Surely?

Nigel thought of Leah's face as he had left that evening. 'Go to your book launch. Just tell me how we're going to pay the fucking mortgage and feed the kids this week,' she had screamed at him down the driveway. She was always like that before her period.

Leah wasn't mean by nature. She had a generous spirit. For

months she had been working on a collection of poetry and liked to toy around with experimental prose. Leah ought to get into greeting cards, he thought. At least they pay. He was getting sick of minding the kids every Tuesday night while she went off to her writing group. Old ladies and retired nuns – what would they know about the art and craft of writing?

She'd been nagging him for days to read her novel. Novel? It was one fucking page. What did she call it? That's right: *The Exile – A Family Saga – Mercifully, Very Short*. Well, thank god for that. And it would have to be about her family, wouldn't it? She was obsessed with her boring bloody family and how she reckoned they'd made her an exile. Not one of her relatives had a cent to bless themselves with anyway. Losers, the bloody lot. Even if they did ask her olds to help with the mortgage, it'd be pointless. He took her precious piece to the toilet. Anything to shut her up. He sat down and started reading.

The Exile – A Family Saga – Mercifully Very Short

The Visit

My good mother arrived with a bag full of absences and reasons why I wasn't invited to the family Christmas, my niece's christening, my brother's wedding and other ancestral gatherings. Couldn't I see it was all my own fault?

My friend arrived with roses in cellophane and bottles of gin.

The Confrontation

You weren't excluded, silly. No one else received invitations, either.
But how did everyone know where to go, or when the wedding was?
Because your brother told them, of course.
So, why was I the only member of the family who wasn't told?
Because you didn't ask.

What Do You Do When They Cast You Out of the Garden?

When you are exiled, you can commit suicide and ask friends to publish your tragic note telling how cruelly your family has treated you. You can have yourself committed, thus becoming a family embarrassment forever. Or like so many others in this situation have done, you could become a writer.

The Choice

Our heroine, who shall remain nameless for legal reasons, chose the latter. At first she found it difficult to make a mark, but once away there was no stopping her. The neighbour in the unit above complained bitterly about the tapping noises in the wee dark hours of the morning.

The Plot Thickens

Our heroine's great literary feat, a self-reflexive work, begins with a chapter very similar to the first chapter of this novel. However, she has the good sense to drink gin with her friend and doesn't waste much time being angst-ridden over the fact that her family couldn't stand her.

Nothing Much More Happens

To hell with legalities, let's give the girl a name. Her name is Penny. Penny just keeps on tapping away, and finds the repetitive act of tap, tap, tapping has a certain Zen. She finally finishes her book, which is extremely defamatory and fortunately for her family is never published.

Not a Happy Ending

Hopefully, dear reader, you have not read the last chapter first. Anyway, in order to create a circular work we must end where we began.

'What do you think?' Leah called through the door.

'Yeah, great, darl, great. Works really well as an outline. But hon, there's no bloody toilet paper. Again!'

The sound of chairs scraping on the polished floorboards gave Sam his cue to follow Nigel to the microphone. Nigel cleared his throat and waited for silence. He liked public speaking. His favourite tactic was to smile and stare at the people in the front row until they were still and then watch as the stillness spread to the rows behind. When all was quiet, he would look down at his feet for about thirty seconds as if he was deciding whether to continue or not, and then he would look up and begin.

He had given some thought to what he was going to say for the launch, but in the end he decided to let Sam's talent and charm speak for itself. Sam in his priest's garb was making an impact. It was clear who the star was.

Clearing his throat, Nigel began, 'Welcome, one and all. I'm not going to bore you with the usual literary claptrap about what a wonderfully talented and handsome chap Sam Clemens is and how he starved for years in order to complete his masterpiece. No, I am simply going to introduce the author and let him tell his own tale. Ladies and gentlemen – I give you Sam Clemens who tonight is launching his first novel, *Infinity and Beyond*. Thank you, Sam.' Nigel handed the microphone to Sam.

Nigel had encouraged him to write this novel. 'You just need a good editor, that's all, Sam,' Nigel had said.

Sam spent about a year, on and off, writing it. Sometimes he'd come home pissed and forlorn, and write into the small hours of the morning, flaking out in a heap at dawn. It was hard to believe that now it had all come to fruition. Yes, he owed Nigel a lot. He'd financed the publishing and even paid for the wine. Nigel had shown great faith.

Sam began by reading from the first chapter. 'This is a book of beginnings. In the beginning, God created the heaven and earth. Earth was waste and empty and the darkness was deep. But then God said let there be light and there was light and it was good. This is a story about light, the reality of light and its binary opposite, darkness. This is a book about creation and about men and women and how they create their realities.'

Sam looked up to see that his mother, who had taken a seat in the front row, was smiling proudly at him. He became aware of cameras flashing. Nigel said to expect this, but not to speak to the press without referring to him first. Don't forget to smile either, Nigel had told him. Sam looked across the audience and smiled, hoping that the diamond in his tooth caught the camera.

He continued. 'Post-modern writers do not impose a fixed ontology or a grand narrative. They offer a view of reality which might resonate with the experience of the reader. In this vein, I hope that I have offered something new, a journey to the underworld to find a treasure. But the treasure won't be my creation. No, in the real self-reflexive sense, it will be the reader's discovery.'

Nigel made his way to the front. 'Thanks to all for coming tonight,' he said. 'Now we'll take a few minutes for any questions that you may like to put to Sam. Yes, the lady in the front.'

'I'd like to ask Mr Clemens who has influenced his work,' asked a woman who looked so tiny in her red beret and tartan skirt that she could have been mistaken for a schoolgirl.

'All the greats, of course – Hemingway, but also Thomas Pynchon, Philip Roth, Paul Auster and of course the wonderful Kurt Vonnegut,' Sam said.

A man with a beard stood up and said, 'Sam, I'd like to ask you about the title and its meaning – *Infinity and Beyond*. How did you come up with the title?'

Sam thought of Nigel's advice – when you're not sure how to answer, look down at your feet for at least ten seconds before replying. It makes the person feel that they may have asked a stupid question and that you are trying not to embarrass them. Smile, say something, anything, and move on quickly. Sam smiled and said, 'Titles tend to suggest themselves.'

A mobile phone rang with the tune of Beethoven's Fifth and its owner rummaged, red-faced, trying to retrieve from the bottom of a very large handbag. Finally the phone stopped and the owner said, 'So sorry, but at least I got your attention,' she laughed. 'My name is Margot and I've got a question for Sam…'

The questions finally faded and Nigel gave Sam the cue to make his way over to the stack of books. He took the microphone and said, 'I'm sure if you purchase a copy of the book this evening you won't be disappointed.'

Sam sat behind the desk, his priestly person framed by thick piles of *Infinity and Beyond*.

A modest queue began to form in front of him. Nigel was taking care of the cash and credit cards. Sam had been practising his signature for weeks, and it had taken on quite a flourish.

'I hope this story intersects with your reality and our worlds collide. Samuel Clemens.'

'That's good. Nice and simple, but memorable,' Nigel had said.

The queue didn't live up to expectations. The initial rush fell away. A few people chatted in small groups, but then began leaving with the smiles that people give when trying to evade people selling raffle tickets in supermarkets.

The last to leave was the little woman in the red beret. She shuffled past the desk, stopping briefly and lifting the cover of a book. 'Good idea, not to pre-sign them, dear,' she said. The sound of her walking stick echoed through the empty hall.

'They drank plenty,' said Sam.

'Yeah, fucking freeloaders,' said Nigel.

The heaviness of disappointment began to descend on them both.

'Could have been the wrong crowd.' Sam ran his hand over the stacks.

Nigel poured himself a large glass of red and drank it down. 'Yeah. Could be.' He counted the takings. 'Two hundred and ninety bucks! We sold ten fucking books.'

'Stay cool, man. What do you think went wrong?' Sam started to feel a lump in this throat.

'Well, that Rasputin get-up for starters. You look like a crazy. The darlings were too scared to come near you.'

'Come on, Nigel. You said I looked good.'

'Well, I lied.' Nigel poured himself another glass of red and knocked it back. 'A thousand fucking books and we sold ten, so we've got nine hundred and ninety left to sell.'

Nigel could picture Leah's tragic face when he told her. 'How am I supposed to buy Easter eggs for the kids?' he could hear her whining. He remembered her last year. 'No Easter eggs again,' she'd yelled.

Hadn't she heard of the childhood obesity epidemic? But it was the symbolism, redemption and rebirth, she'd cried. What was life if you didn't honour symbols and rituals? So he wouldn't bloody tell her the books didn't sell. No way.

'The bookshops will take some.'

'Yeah, they'll take some but not the whole nine hundred and ninety. We got three hundred people here. We should have sold three hundred books. Face facts, Sam. You scared them off.' Nigel poured more wine. His nose was red and shining and he'd slopped wine all over his pants.

Sam thought about telling him that his fly was undone but decided against it. 'Thought the money wasn't all that important to you. You said to believe Woody Allen – you know, "eighty per cent of success is showing up". You said the most important thing about art was to get it out there.'

'Man, if it was art!' Nigel picked up a book from the stack and hurled it against the wall. 'A good cover designed by me. A good blurb written by me and a whole lot of shit in between.' Nigel swigged the bottle. His cheeks had taken on a purple tinge. 'I would've been better off publishing Leah's fucking poetry, Nigel thought. 'You owe me three thousand bucks, man.' Nigel knocked the pile of books of the desk, sending them flying. He lurched towards the door taking a bottle of opened red with him.

Tears were running down Sam's face now, the kohl around his eyes smudged so that under the glare of the fluorescent light his face he looked a bit like that of a snowman. 'But Nigel, you can keep the books, man,' Sam called after him. He heard the loud revving of a car. 'Oh yeah, Nige,' he yelled, 'someone said there's a booze bus on the corner...'

Maybe Something More

To: Worthy Writers Group
From: Margot@not.com

Hi, All,

Workshopping time again. Here is my story for the month. I wrote it after attending the Breakthrough workshop I told you all about. I look forward to your feedback, which is always so stimulating.

Best, Margot

Something More

Leah took a seat by the door. She was just in time for the introductions. She was surprised at the number of men in the group. One had already published a novel, apparently, at least two were studying a Masters of Creative Writing and another had travelled from Darwin for the session. The women seemed to be the usual bunch of retired schoolteachers, hopeful young students, lesbians and mothers looking for something more.

When it came to her turn to introduce herself, she felt vaguely fraudulent. It had been over a year since she had written anything of substance. She muttered something about hoping this workshop would cure her writer's block.

Tobias began his talk, breathing long sweeping sentences with the same rhythm you might find in a Hemingway story. 'The short story is defined by its exclusiveness – by what it doesn't say, rather than by what it does.' His deep melodic American tone filled Leah with hope. His feet were crossed neatly under the desk. He was wearing navy blue sneakers with white ripple soles, and his features were handsome in an almost movie matinee film star way.

Leah felt that if she could have combed some black hair dye through his wavy locks, he would have looked just like a young Elvis. Tobias Fargo would be the one to lead her from the wilderness.

He sat at an angle to the desk like the big hand of the clock at five minutes to the hour. 'The short story,' he said, 'Should contain a moment of profound revelation. Its reader should be different than they were before they read the story. It should be sparse in text but rich in meaning. There is very little oxygen to spare in the short story form.'

Leah needed to be reminded of her love for tight, superbly written prose.

'The short story should be like a very long poem. And it should contain something precious that the reader can take with them. But what of this precious thing – what is it and why should the reader care?' said Tobias.

The feedback writers give each other is pure gold, Leah had once heard a fellow writer say. Pure gold could be both extremely helpful and extremely dangerous, and was always to be taken with the proverbial pinch of salt, Leah thought. Feedback, criticism, revision, call it what you will, are external to the writer and in a sense are forms of rewriting, reworking of the original form. Writing was her art, her expression, her creation, her therapy. Leah was always very careful about who she allowed to read and critique her work. It wasn't that she was sensitive – far from it. Nigel had cured her of that. No, it was just that misunderstanding of her work disappointed her profoundly. Some might call this arrogance, an unwillingness to assume professional detachment. Others might consider that resistance to the input of others is essential to the soul of the artist.

Leah both sought and rejected reaction to her work, like a perverse woman might seek and reject the attention of the opposite sex. For months Leah had only been able to scratch away at bits of flash fiction and the odd poem. Her poems never really seemed to hit the mark with those who listened. Sometimes her poetry was an apology for not writing decent prose. Recently, she had read the term *poete maudit* in a literary dictionary and decided that the term had a forlorn ring to it, and that a *poete maudit* was something she didn't want to be. So she had returned to her prose, the short story in particular, thinking that if she had to fail as a writer she would prefer to fail as a short story writer than as a poet.

Tobias Fargo's short story workshop was advertised as a writer's opportunity for a breakthrough. Just what every writer is looking for at some stage of their career – a breakthrough, thought Leah when she read the advertisement. After this workshop maybe she would find within herself that story she had been seeking for so long.

Tobias asked the group to think about James Joyce's *The Dead*. 'Why,' asked Tobias, 'are we willing to accept that snow falling can be "heard", when, rationally we know that snow falls silently?'

'Is it that the short story form should be capable of leading the reader to some kind of epiphany? You know, it was Joyce who glamorised this term,' Leah said.

Tobias looked down at the desk as if he was profoundly embarrassed or deeply moved. Leah noticed that his hair parting was slightly crooked. He held his head in this position for so long that Leah wondered if he had gone to sleep.

Finally he raised his head, looked out of the window and said in his long sweeping way, 'I think the power of the story lies in its ending. The resolution should bring all the forces of the character's life to bear so that the character, and perchance the reader, realises something outside themselves, something more.'

'Something for which there is perhaps no language?' said Leah.

Tobias frowned at Leah and then quickly smiled at the group. 'It is important that all participants get an opportunity to comment. It becomes difficult if one person dominates. We will write for an hour without a break and then we will share our work,' said Tobias.

This was a tall order – writing for a solid hour. It was a rare event for Leah to have the opportunity to write uninterrupted for an hour. Most of her writing was done in opportunistic snatches, while waiting to pick up children from soccer, or when a DVD was so engrossing that no one asked her where their socks were or what was to eat. The last time she wrote for an hour at a stretch was while she was waiting in the hospital waiting room when her son had broken his arm.

Leah picked up her pen and gazed around the room. All of the group were writing with such intensity, it was as if they had come already prepared with a story and all they were doing was transcribing it on to paper.

After what seemed like just a few minutes, Tobias was calling for the first volunteer to read their work. The young man from Darwin began.

Leah watched him. His complexion seemed so fair and soft for one from the tropics, and his hands so small and white, delicate almost. Nigel, her husband's, were yellow and nicotine-stained, and his nails bitten. The young man wrote about lonely bars, heavily made-up women with broken teeth and cigarette breath, drunken nights and seedy hotel rooms. His beard didn't entirely cover the soft, rosy boyishness of his cheeks. Leah felt she wanted to kiss his cheek like a mother kisses a child after a bad dream in the night, and tell him that it would all be all right. His story ended with 'He didn't know how much longer he could stand it.' What was it about this maleness of suffering? Leah mused. Men suffer differently from women, almost crucifixion style, she thought. There was nobility to it. An aspect of classical tragedy, she thought.

Tobias praised the sparse minimalism of the young writer's descriptions. 'Yes,' he said, 'it is hard when you leave a place because you can no longer stay where you are, and you expect everything to be different in the new place. But it isn't – you are still the same person, with the same problems – just in a different place, knowing no one and no one knowing you. That can be hard.'

The next writer was a woman wearing a baseball hat and a leather vest. She wrote of trips to South America and nights out with arty friends. Her drunken female protagonist said, 'I hope some of these young guys might see me as a mother they might want to fuck – you know, like Oedipus and they can be mother-fuckers and who will I be? Will I be a fucked mother?'

Leah thought well, yes, maybe a bit strong but she liked the Oedipus idea. Tobias suggested that the writer still had to find the 'soul' of the story.

Finally it was Leah's turn to read. She looked down at her notebook. She felt happy about this story – it had just come. They are always the best stories – the ones that just come. She remembered years ago watching a cooking show where a chef demonstrated the correct way to peel an egg. He had demonstrated two eggs – one done in the professional way where the shell just fell off, revealing a perfectly smooth surface, and another which looked lumpy, picked at and with bits of shell hanging off it. Stories are like that, she thought. Sometimes you can work away for months at a piece and it still doesn't come together. At other times the story will just reveal itself as smoothly as a professionally peeled egg. She cleared her throat.

'It's not exactly a story – more an impression or an attempt at abstract prose.'

Tobias looked up, glanced at the clock. 'No need to explain. Just read the story. We are running short of time.'

'Okay. Sorry. Hear goes.' Leah cleared her throat again and began reading.

Detachment: A Triptych

Disappointment

Disappointment has a turquoise hue lending a little more towards green than blue, and shimmers with a yellow aura. Its texture is somewhat rough, similar to the feel of a tweed jacket against the inside of your wrist or a jute floor rug underfoot. Salty to the taste, disappointment has a slightly bitter resonance and a musty smell a little like mould. It has a hollow sound, like that of a rubbish can being tapped with a teaspoon.

Disillusionment

Disillusionment has been likened to cynicism, but I think disenchantment is a kinder and less judgemental simile suggesting that the former state had been one of enchantment. Its deep blue hue, midnight blue in fact, blurs at the edges suggesting shadows and mist. Disillusionment echoes softly. Sometimes described as having a deceptively smooth texture which becomes sticky over time, it is generally tasteless and smells like stale smoke.

Despair

Despair is predictably dark in colour with high saturation and low value. Its hue varies with the depth of the state. Deep despair takes on an

aubergine aspect, usually with a matt finish, non-reflective and dull, like
the surface of early black figure Greek pottery. Despair sounds like a
badly tuned piano and feels like metal filings under fingernails. It smells
like gas with a hint of carbon monoxide. As you would expect, despair
has a most peculiar taste and it is different for each individual. Those who
are religious tell us that despair in any form is unpalatable.

Leah looked up at Tobias. He was staring down at the desk. She
noticed that not only was his hair parting crooked, but that there was a
glisten of grey hairs amongst the gold. Leah was about to cough when
he finally looked up.

'Would anyone like to offer any comments about this work?'

The woman in the baseball cap broke the silence. 'It could be
poetry but it isn't. It's prose, but not narrative. I'm not sure how you
would classify this type of writing. All I know is that I don't like it.'

'I agree,' said the young man with the small white hands and red
beard. 'I couldn't engage with it all. These emotions are so different
for each person but the descriptions are like something from a science
textbook.'

'But that was the whole…' Leah spluttered.

'Yes,' said Tobias. 'Virginia Woolf was criticised for her detached
style, and detachment has its place. But your prose, as well as being
detached, is an attempt at the abstract in the same manner as a visual
artist might paint the emotions. Am I right?'

'Yes, more or less. It is an experiment really.'

'Experiment it may be. It just doesn't work.'

A young man with dreadlocks who hadn't spoken before said, 'I
don't know why you have all those tentative adverbs like "generally"
and "predictably". Why don't you just punch it out – personalise the
whole thing. Surely, you're not suggesting that there is such a thing as
generic emotion? I mean, generic despair is drawing a pretty long bow.'

People began to make more suggestions.

Tobias interrupted. 'I would like to make just one more comment
if I may. Writing a story is like any artistic creative act. It arises from

inspiration but requires the artist's imagination and talent to develop into something more. The result is relative to the degree to which the artist possesses these qualities. In fact, I don't agree with the premise that success is more or less a matter of just showing up. I think that success comes from something much more than just showing up.'

'But,' said Leah, 'sometimes untalented people succeed – especially untalented men.'

Leah was thinking of a recent launch her husband had been involved in. He had funded the publishing of one his student's novels. It had been a disaster. But the student had eventually managed to sell all of the one thousand books her husband had paid to have printed and had kept all of the money. Leah had hated the novel and thought that it was garbage. The student used the profits from the sale of the first to self-publish another and now a mainstream publisher had made him an offer. But Leah regretted her comment immediately. Clearly by the flush on Tobias's face, he had taken it personally.

'I didn't mean...'

Tobias glanced again at the clock. 'We have just a few minutes left, so to wind up I will read a few pages from my latest story, "What I Did When I Found the Holy Grail". He began reading.

Leah wasn't listening. She thought of yesterday when she had shown Nigel her new poetry. He had suggested that she try to make some extra money writing greeting cards. Greeting cards! He had no respect for her work. At times she felt he had no respect for her either. But he was obsessed with his own work, constantly asking her to read his chapters, to listen to his boring plots. He even nagged her to write his grant applications. The unemployment payment went directly into his account. He was the keeper and she, as his spouse, was unable to claim anything separately. That's the way it is. He gave her what he thought was enough for the food, but it never was. And now he had committed all that money to that kid's pathetic novel. The only way out was for her to get a job, put the kids in childcare and he would stay home and write. She would become the 'long-suffering wife of the struggling writer'. She would make the sacrifice. Never again to see her children's faces forlorn and disappointed at Easter time when the only Easter eggs she had to give them were boiled eggs she had painted herself with food dye. Kids just weren't that into symbolism. Yes, she would make the sacrifice. Maybe.

Margot turned on her computer, wondering what reactions to *Something More* might be waiting for her. She always had to steel herself for this monthly task of reading the email responses of her fellow writers.

Earlier in the day, she had been to see her accountant. Accountants, she mused, are generally such nice people – innocents almost. Not for them the strain and labouring over the nuances of words, obsessing over shades of meaning, stealing details from the lives of their friends and family and then claiming that everything they write is fiction. Writers are the carrion of the art world.

To: Margot@not.com
From: Louise

Loved your story. I do suspect, however, that your male protagonist is a bit of a wank. Sometimes, Margot, I think that you don't think much of male writers. Got to watch that, you know. It can sometimes sound like sour grapes. Louise

To: Margot@not.com
From: Paul

Poets have trouble with prose sometimes (and I am a poet after all.) There are parts of this that I really liked but I do suggest that you condense it a little. Can't help but wonder who is really telling the story and why. Cheers, Peter

To: Margot@not.com
From: Nyall

Hi, Margot

The problem with your story is that it doesn't really make much sense. Even so, I liked it and I'm not really sure why. I think you are

headed for a quest. Do you know what is it is that you are looking for?
XX Nyall

To: Margot@not.com
From: Joan

Hi, Mez

I'm not sure about the story. Not sure if you're taking the piss or not. But on the whole I liked it. I think you need to keep working on it.

Joan

To: Margot@not.com
From: Alex

Margot, as always your story has merit and in parts it is excellent. But it needs something more.

Your friend, Alex

Yes, Alex was her friend, and as always he was right.

Homage to Eveline

Louise gazed absently out of the kitchen window as she peeled the hard-boiled eggs. She was vaguely aware that the venetian blind was dusty. She was tired. The shell had stuck to the eggs and they looked lumpy and picked at. Things like this were important to her. Details. Her life had become a mass of small details important to nobody much, except her. Still, she was chopping the eggs up to go in a salad – her husband wouldn't notice that they weren't smooth. He wouldn't have noticed anyway. To him, food was food. To him, good table manners meant eating your food off a plate.

She thought of the way Norm would hold his knife and fork and while he was chewing he would rest his fists on the table, knife and fork upwards, tomato sauce bottle next to his plate on the left, salt shaker on the right. Years in the plumbing trade had given him hands like boxing gloves. After tea, he would settle in front of the television, recliner extended and watch the news and sport and drink beer until he dozed off.

Louise had called her friend Margot late one evening.

'Louise, be sensible. You can't leave Norm now. Where would you go? Where would you live? What would you do? You'd just end up more alone than you are now, and a hell of a lot poorer. No one wants women our age – not even our kids. Just be happy with what you've got.'

In his way, Norm was a handsome man and when her friends visited, if he made an effort, he could be quite engaging. He would tell a funny story and they would laugh. He would wink at them and they seemed to like him. When he chatted to her friends she sometimes felt she had disappeared almost entirely. Norm did a lot of plumbing work for women, single women, women who enjoyed having a man to chat to, to make morning tea for. Coffee in a thick mug, with biscuits on a saucer on the side. Maybe an offer of a fresh sandwich for lunch, with a slice of orange cake. Another cup of coffee? Some women love to please a man. She herself did, after all, didn't she? Didn't she realise how fortunate she was to have him? And he had been faithful to her. 'Nothing lower than a man who cheats on his wife, Louise. You've got nothing to worry about with me on that score.'

Sometimes in the evenings she would put on a dress, sit with him in the lounge room and have a glass of wine. She would try and talk about things that interested him, but the conversation would soon fade away and he would become mesmerised by something on the television. She would take her notebook and pencil, go and sit on the porch and write her lies.

It wasn't that there wasn't any conversation. He would always ask her about her day, and if he was in good mood or feeling guilty about something he would give her a hug and try to kiss her. She would always turn her cheek. She never wanted him to kiss her on the mouth. Even that degree of intimacy with him was over, for her. When the kids were still living at home she would pretend. No need to now. She would ask him about his day and he would tell her, briefly. When the youngest had left, she thought she wouldn't survive. In the evenings after Norm had dozed off, the silence was thick and hung around her like a shroud.

It was her fiction writing that saved her, made it possible to believe that all was not lost, that maybe her soul had not shrivelled and died, not completely anyway. She could have a life of sorts, if only in her imagination.

Imagination was something that Norm did not understand unless it was imagining a woman without her clothes like he sometimes did when he was watching television. She's all right. Big around the rump, but she'd do me on a dark night. Or what he was going to do when he won ten thousand on a trifecta.

Louise had all but given up discussing her imaginings with him. She thought of the conversation they had had last Boxing Day when they went out for a drive. The motion of the car had relaxed her. They had been driving in silence for some time. She had let her guard down, forgot who she was talking to. She told him how she had bumped into some mutual friends who were renovating an old property out of town, and how they had joked about a ghost who was rumoured to be in the house. Louise had told them how she had seen a ghost sitting in a chair under the pear tree when she and Norm had visited them last.

Norm held the steering wheel of the car in the same way he held his knife and fork. 'You told them you saw a ghost?' he asked her.

She began to explain how she hadn't actually physically seen one, but had felt the presence of one. She was only part way through her explanation when he erupted.

'Why the hell are you always making up stupid fucking stories? Why are you always telling lies?'

Her reply was stuck in her throat like Snow White's apple. She spluttered, struggled to get out the words. 'Because…because I'm a writer – that's what I do. I make up stories. Fuckhead. I make up stories to survive.'

That was the end of the drive.

That night she lay on top of the bed and didn't close her eyes once.

Norm suggested that she take an aspirin. 'Louise, darl, if you can't see something, it just isn't there. There's nothing under the pear tree but dog shit.'

She'd written a few good stories lately – sent them off to the usual literary magazines. No success. Most of what seemed to be published by younger women writers was smart and snappy– not much dialogue, not much emotion, not much about the everyday stuff of life. She discussed this with her writing friends.

Margot said, 'They think our stories have all been told. They don't want to know about home and hearth, loving and caring any more. They want hard-edged females – thinkers, intellectual – like men.'

Louise had known Margot for a while. She was a great one to workshop stories with.

'You know, Louise, I heard a woman on the radio only yesterday, a young woman. She reckoned that if a man wrote about family and life it would be considered universal, but if a woman wrote about the same thing it would relegated to chick lit or special interest. What you've got to do, Louise, is write like a man, think like a man and then they'll publish you. You should know by now it's a man's world.'

'Yeah, but "a woman's work is never done", so I'm just going to keep on writing like a woman.'

'Love your clichés, Louise, don't you? Careful you don't become one.'

Louise was struggling with her latest story. She was trying to illustrate the difficulty of being an older woman writer in a world of smart young things, particularly smart young men, but at the same time giving her characters dimension. Sometimes she felt her characters, especially her male characters, weren't characters at all but caricatures. It was the most difficult part of writing, getting that character just right. Louise sometimes had to check herself because her research sometimes involved striking up conversations with complete strangers just to find a word or an idiosyncrasy for one her characters. Lately she noticed she had fewer and fewer non-writing friends. Maybe some of her old friends were finding her an embarrassment. Not quite who she used be.

Going to university had helped her get over the kids leaving home. She especially enjoyed studying the Modernist writers. The lecturer was a small-framed, humble man who wore a tweed jacket whatever the temperature, and who spoke with a semi-English accent which so many of the male lecturers seemed to have. He had written a PhD on James Joyce's *Dubliners*. For the final assignment he asked students to write about any one of Joyce's stories in the collection. Louise chose 'Eveline'. There had been much discussion in the classroom about it. Most students seemed to think that the character Eveline lacked the courage to leave her impoverished life, that if only she had shown a bit more grit she could have taken up the offer of a new life with Frank in Buenos Aires. She could have left her miserable existence and the dusty cretonne curtains behind.

Louise's assignment was titled 'In Defence of Eveline'. She wrote,

> Joyce left Eveline gripping the iron railing, paralysed, unable to leave, chained to her misery like an ill-treated dog unable to leave its cruel master. The point of Joyce's story is that Eveline couldn't leave. For a multitude of reasons the only real choice she had was to stay. The cruelty and misery of her situation is highlighted by this offer of escape, an offer which caused Eveline great internal conflict. She longed for the love of a man, for a new life, but when the time came to board the boat she just couldn't go.
>
> Had Eveline left with Frank for Buenos Aires she would have to live with the guilt of having abandoned her younger siblings and of having broken a promise to her dying mother. How could you Eveline? How could you betray your promise to your dead mother? For shame Eveline. To abandon your poor father and leave your little brothers and sisters to fend for themselves. Shame on you. May God forgive for what you have done, Eveline.
>
> Even if it were possible for her to return to Ireland in the future for a visit, she would not have been welcomed back in her homeland. She would have been an outcast forever more. I think that Eveline had the imagination to know she wouldn't survive. I consider that Eveline was trapped in a social bind between a rock and a hard place, between the devil and the deep blue sea and in the end she chose the devil she knew, and that in itself took courage. God bless you, Eveline. I salute you and your courage.

The lecturer had spoken kindly to Louise when he handed back her assignment. He found it hard to believe that she was serious, and she really must desist from using common figures of speech when writing a conclusion to an academic essay, especially an essay about the work of Joyce, who was a master of the English language and who would have been outraged by her use of clichés and trivial idiom. He had, however, awarded her a lower pass.

Her son had a friend who used to visit occasionally. Sometimes, he would sit next to her on the couch and ask her to help him with his essays. How old was he? Twenty, maybe twenty-one? Or was he seventeen? How old was she? Fifty something. Disgusting. She disgusted herself. Even Louise's own imaginings couldn't permit such a thing. She knew his mother. Hard-faced practical woman. But he was not hard-faced or practical. He had long wavy hair, wore an indigo velvet jacket and studied literature. Once, in a whisper, he recited Keats to her: 'My heart aches, and a drowsy numbness pains / My sense, as though of hemlock I had drunk', and softly, barely touched the inside of her wrist with his lips. He knew what she knew. He recognised what she recognised. He muttered, 'Sorry,' and left. He never visited again. There was an ocean between them.

What would have happened if she had crossed the ocean to this young poet? Who in her world would stand for a fifty-something mother of four from the suburbs running off with a young man of twenty; or was he seventeen? She could hear Norm's reaction. 'Stupid little poofter. Stoned out of his brain most of the time. God, he'd get a hell of a shock when he sobered up and found himself next to you and your saggy old tits, Louise. That'd sure teach the dirty little bastard a lesson. They ought to throw you in the slammer, Louise. Fooling around with little boys.' Her exile would have been absolute, just like Evaline's. Banished from the garden forever.

She remembered one of her friends had a crush on her father for years. Her entire family, especially her mother, thought it was a huge joke. For Evelyn, with the young poet, it wasn't a physical thing – not a lustful thing. Or maybe it was. Once he had showed her a piece he had written. He had read it to her so earnestly.

Breathless: On a warm summer's night you stand there shining your new hair-do dark and slicked down over your brow metal regaling your lips and diamonds in your teeth so sweetly you smile silk scarf at your throat you hold the butcher man's door open wide so I can come inside and buy red meat for my soul you say softly that meat is good for your heart blood is good for your soul as you take my hand and kiss the veins on the inside of my wrist white and thin white and thin was Marie Antoinette's neck as she knelt with her head on the block white and thin till the blood fell and the blood ran thick blood is good for heart you say death is good for the soul.

She had seen the young would-be Keats in a café in the city a few months back. He didn't recognise her, or if he did he didn't let on. He seemed unaware of anyone, his head bent over his coffee, scribbling, shoulders hunched. His long legs were stretched under the table so she could see the worn soles of his boots, jeans tattered at the ankles and ripped at the knees. Thin wrists, strong elegant hands to hold the pen chewed at the end. Wanted no one. Needed no one. He had everything he needed. He wore his singularity like a crown.

Not like Louise. She had come to the café to drink coffee and write but she had not yet mastered the nonchalant persona of a person confident enough to sit alone. Louise felt that if she bumped into people she knew, she had to offer some explanation for why she was sitting alone in a café. She felt a kind of shame – the shame of being by herself. She had a rehearsed speech just in case. 'I'm just waiting for Norm to finish his business or I'm waiting for a friend but maybe they got the date mixed up.'

But as a young woman she loved sitting alone in coffee shops. She smoked then, and she felt sophisticated. It was cool to be pale-faced, a mystery alone, smoking and doing nothing in particular. Someone nearly always sat down and talked to her, but never a young poet in an indigo velvet jacket. A handsome plumber's apprentice sat down one day and asked her if she had a light. 'Life is but a cigarette,' he said. Perhaps he was right.

Louise heard the familiar sound of the gravel crunching as the van with Norm's 'Friendly Home Plumbing' painted on the side pulled into the driveway. She watched him though the window as he got out of the car and walked over to speak to the neighbour who was watering her roses, her long brown legs glistening in the late afternoon sun. Louise watched him lean against the fence and reach across to take a leaf from the neighbour's hair. He was laughing, relaxed, unaware of her observing him through the dusty venetians. His demeanour was not unlike that of her young poet – absorbed in the conversation, confident in his stance. But Norm wasn't waiting for an epiphany to find out who he was, or what he wanted. He had always known.

Eventually he made his way through the back door. 'Jesus, Louise what's that pong? Smells like a Chinaman's dunny in here.'

The egg shells had piled up in the kitchen sink. Louise peeled the last egg and the shell came away cleanly, almost whole, revealing a perfectly formed egg, glossy and white, surface as smooth as an ancient marble statue.

Letter from Virginia

Virginia Woolf & Co.
Room of One's Own
Utopia Somewhere

Dear Margot and friends,

Can I call you girls? In some ways, I would rather call you that, than women writing 'in my shadow'. The image of the shadow concerns me somewhat. Do I cast a shadow? I would rather shed light. The way out, as I wrote nearly a hundred years ago, is to earn money and to have a room of your own. It was the only way then, and it is the only way now. I urge you and plead with you to do it. If you stay with the self-serving stereotypes who masquerade as you husbands, you are doomed. You will never fulfil your potential as a human beings, let alone as a writers. Once you are women of independent means, you can do with them as you will. Dispense with him, or keep him a pet if you feel the need. Once you are independent, he will be rendered harmless, if not useless. Did I not write years ago, 'I need not hate any man; he cannot hurt me. I need not flatter any man, he has nothing to give me.' Persist, my dears, persist.

Now, a word of warning. Be careful my dears, not to take on the role of victim. You can always use what seems an intolerable situation to your advantage; you turn your suffering into art, and this is always a positive move. You may not actually have a room of your own in which to write, but psychologically and emotionally you do. Your vagina is your own now, is it not? Some of you may have a husband called Norm – and indeed he does seem to be the norm for many of his generation – who has no need of that part of you any more. (He might struggle in that area himself. Rather than let you know, it is better for him for you to think that you are no longer attractive, and how could he be expected to rise to the occasion for someone like you.) But let me tell you, you are all still very attractive, no matter what your age. If your vagina is currently vacant, what are you waiting for?

And as for you, Margot. Where are you? You are weaving in and out of the text, hiding behind words and phrases like a frightened child hides behind her mother's skirt. Who are you? You must come out and declare yourself. You are the author, the writer of stories, are you not? And yet you render yourself almost invisible. Why? You intrigue me with this little book you have produced. Clearly it contains your own work, but what is its purpose? Do you plan to leave it lying around in coffee shops and libraries, in the hope that some passing stranger will come by and read it and declare you a genius? Do you imagine this imaginary reader will say then, 'I must contact Margot immediately and offer her a book contract'? Margot, get real! Even if they did appreciate your work, it is so unclear who you are and where you can be contacted that it just wouldn't happen. Why have you not put your name and number in big clear letters on the cover? Why aren't you sending your precious manuscript to publishers with letters of shameless self-promotion? Why, Margot, do you try to erase yourself? You do this even in your own fiction. And I must comment on the title of this little work – *Heart Jottings*. Really, Margot, you can do better. It reminds me of bird droppings.

I must ask you about your character Louise, who spends a lot time looking out the window. I too had characters who stared out the window like Louise does. Mrs Dalloway, for example, on the night of her famous party, spent time staring out the window. Orlando's biographer suggests that 'the only resource now left us is to look out the window'. For my characters, the act of looking out the window is, in a manner of speaking, a little like looking into a crystal ball. They are given a glimpse of the future. But what does your character

Louise see through her window? Her odious husband lurching after the neighbour. You don't reveal her inner epiphany at that moment, but I hope she realises what she must do. My advice to your character Louise is simply this: dump him.

All of you must all realise the work you do as women in the home is not as arduous as it once was. You don't scrub away at blackened pans, pound bread or labour over piles of washing on Mondays. Your workload is far less than that of working-class women one hundred years ago. I'm not saying that for today's working-class women, life is without drudgery. No. But it is nowhere near as hard as the lives of your great grandmothers, as perhaps the life of Jimmy Joyce's Eveline. For many women of your great grandmother's and grandmother's time, even if they were literate, a writing life would have been completely out of the question. No, it is not so bad for you now.

I urge you all to follow your writing path with determination and belief. Only 'slip off your petticoats when it suits you'. Do not hide behind your sitting room's doors stealing a few minutes when you can. Take all the time you need to pursue your art, follow up every educational opportunity that comes your way, earn your own money, stand up to your critics. Don't despair as I did. I deeply regret that my suicide note didn't explain more. Believe in yourselves but, above all else, have courage.

Ever Yours

 Virginia

Email to Virginia

To: Virginia@utopiasomewhere.com
From: Margot@not.com
Subject: The Write of Reply

Dear Virginia

I feel compelled to respond as you seem to have singled me out in your letter. I am assuming that this is because I am the author, albeit a fictitious one. Firstly, please let me bring you up to date with the present situation as I see it.

Virginia, you are no longer the lone voice in the wilderness that you once were. Since your passing, social conditions have improved greatly for women. You seemed to foresee this in *A Room of One's Own*. I'm sure you would find the French theories of the feminine interesting. These are often referred to under the label of *écriture féminine*. Some find the cluster of ideas that gather under this heading quite complex and dense, but essentially it refers to women being in touch with their bodies through language that empowers the specifically feminine.

Although, myself, I do wonder about how such theorising and nebulous abstraction advances the position of women and in particular women writers myself. Certainly, it calls the patriarchal dominant system to account for their oppressive practices, but do oppressors ever care about the negative consequences of their oppression on those whom they oppress?

Speaking of masculine supremacy, you have asked me about my own circumstances. Well, my position once resembled the one of Jane Eyre who seemed to escape from one form of captivity to another. But now I live alone. Alone in a housing ministry one-bedroom unit in Short Gully, just near Sparrowhawk in central Victoria. No, Virginia, I am not married to a solicitor or a successful businessman. I am not kept, so to speak. I am not rich. But I have my freedom, a room of my own and enough to live on – just. I guess you might say that I was working class when I was married, but now I am just below that, in what you might call the surviving class. It is still not easy being a single older woman, especially one who writes. I am – and I know you would approve – studying at uni to complete an Arts degree. The very best I can hope for is that it will lead me to the financial support of a scholarship which will allow me to write my fiction. And, as you so astutely pointed out, I am hiding behind the door with my writing. If I am honest, I guess I am just plain scared. A degree might give me the confidence and courage I seem to lack – perhaps.

Virginia, it's not really all that great being an older single woman with only a bit of money and a shabby little room in which to write. You predicted that women would cease to be the protected sex and that we would take part in all the activities and exertions that we were once excluded from. You wrote, 'The nursemaid will heave coal. The shop woman will drive an engine.' Yes, this is now, in fact, so. Many things have changed for women but some things have stayed the same. I'm sorry to have to tell you that patriarchy is still alive and well.

What perhaps is different is that there are now many women writers and feminist critics who, like yourself, resist the dominant patriarchal voice in literature. It is true that in the past women have had no real place in literature, other than as idealist constructs based on concepts of good or bad depending on how the female character helps or hinders male practices. However, and I know you'll be pleased about this, the current discourse has created an awareness of the position of women in both literature and the literary world.

Virginia, I don't know what you think, but I feel that the writing of stories, stories with female characters who are from the working class, will do more to advance women's position in society than the Franco-feminists' theories, because such stories would be accessible to more women than are the writings of academic theorists. That might sound a bit arrogant, but you are encouraging me to be more confident, aren't you? But please don't get the idea that I don't admire the work of the theorists. It's just that I sometimes think they might be sitting in ivory towers somewhere, no kids, no husbands or husbands who earn a mint – you know the type. I can imagine them in Paris apartments, with white billowy curtains and embroidered satin cushions scattered on plush couches.

Here, I must confess my Marxist leanings – social conditions are a greater influence than gender, in some respects. But you probably think that's just sour grapes on my part. Speaking of sour grapes, that reminds me: before I go, I must tell you about Germaine Greer, who was born in the year of your death. She published *The Female Eunuch* in 1970 and it created such a stir. Germaine has done much to give women a voice. I am sure that you would like her writing very much.

One final thing. The other day I workshopped a piece of fiction in a class which seemed a bit male-dominated. I read my latest piece. They all hated it! They said my narrator was way too harsh. Any way, here it is:

Vignette

It was one of those days, you know, those shut-down days, those grey wizened, chilly wind, no birds singing days. In front of me, along the path, two telegraph poles away, a man, middle-aged at least, stopped dead in his stride, turned and hugged the slim hooded figure next to him. Radiant heat from the hug warmed me, fleetingly. Second wife. Would have to be the second wife. Ten years younger than him. I'll just bet she is.

Closer now, only one telegraph pole away. He must be fifty, maybe more. Baggy green cords ballooning in the wind, he holds the hug and kisses the loved one's head. The hood, silky-lined, slides down from a crop of silver hair. Not trophy wife after all. Getting closer. Could it be first wife? No, too old. Mother, maybe?

Upon them now. No. It's not second wife, first wife or mother. The kissed one, the hugged one, the loved one is a small, frail, silver-haired old man, walking frame resting on the kerb.

Feeling strangely warmed, privileged even to have witnessed this version of love and to be reminded that true love takes many forms. I walk on past a shop where I used to work. The glass front is pasted up, newspapers, yellowed and peeling. There is a small sign on the door. 'Re-opening for business soon'.

Well, Virginia, I thought this was all right – I still do. One fellow really took exception to my comments about the second wife. Oh well, I will persist.

Well, that just about completes my update. Thank you for your encouragement. At the beginning of *A Room of One's Own* you tell us so wisely, 'A woman must have money and a room of her own if she is to write fiction.' Yes, Virginia, it has always been thus.

Warmest regards

Margot

PS I have taken on board what you said about my book, *Heart Jottings*. You know, someone did actually ring me the other day – someone from the council. I thought they were going to offer me a job or a grant. But, no. The man, who said he was from environmental health, told me that if I kept leaving these books lying around the town I could be charged with littering. But I will not be changing the title. I like it.

Heart Jottings

Missing

Today I missed you. I missed you yesterday too, but today I missed you more. I'm not sure why. Maybe it was because it was raining. Early this morning the sun was shining but then it clouded over and started to drizzle. The soft misty rain continued for most of the day. It stopped for a short time around midday, so I went to sit in the garden under the autumn tree and ate my cheese sandwich. But just as I finished eating it started to rain softly, and softly rain so I went back inside and stared out the window for a while. I listened to my new Nick Cave CD. I played it three times and then I decided to take my dog for a walk. The air outside smelled fresh and the rain on my face mixed with tears of missing you. Some days I miss you more than others – it's hard to know why that is really. Missing you is a hard thing to quantify. I guess it's just that some days ache more than others.

Later, when I came back from my walk, I played Nick Cave again. The phone rang once and for some reason I thought it might be you, but of course it wasn't. It was still raining softly and softly raining at tea time, but it didn't matter because I wasn't going out anywhere. I decided to skip dinner and sat down and watched the news and the weather report. Apparently it will be raining again tomorrow and the next day and the day after that.

Today I missed you and I will miss you tomorrow and all the days after that and all the days after that.

Love Jacket

Pieta slipped on the jacket and in soft surprise became instantly warm. She was caught unawares by the gentle warmth of the silk lining caressing her bare arms, enveloping her in a feeling of such tenderness and poignancy that she was unable to speak. Aglow, she allowed the sensation to enfold and engulf her with all of its wondrous intensity.

It was as if an angel had wrapped her in his wings – soft loving white angel wings. Had she ever felt this way before? Maybe a little this way with Joe, but no, this was different, as gentle as mist, as light as a baby's smile. She pulled the jacket closer to her.

George and Alison had forgotten she was there; in the shadows they were like the figures in the Rodin sculpture – kissing with the sublime forgetfulness of lovers and dreamers. Behind them the hot summer sun set in rosy blaze.

Tristesse

Vincent Van Gogh's *Still Life: Vase with Fifteen Sunflowers* hung on the wall of the solicitor's waiting room, the same print that had hung above the king-sized bed in the honeymoon suite where her marriage had begun fifteen years ago. Then it had seemed to her a cheerful scene – a bunch of yellow flowers in a vase.

The tortuous yellow flowers had born silent witness to their clumsy lovemaking in those early hopeful days and it seemed almost prophetic to her that the picture should re-appear in her life at this moment. Fifteen flowers. Each flower so different, contorted and misshapen in an expression of discrete anguish, yet together the flowers formed a perfect composition. She stared at the picture and thought how each wretched flower could be a representation of each year of her marriage – a composition most imperfect.

The sunflowers are ravaged, she thought. You can almost hear them screaming their agonies. She remembered learning at school how Van Gogh had loved yellow, how he saw it as a symbol of light both within and without the human heart. But his sunflowers are not really yellow, she thought – more mustard – variations of many different shades of mustard – such a cold and piteous colour.

Venus

She carried the tray back to the bedroom. Jim had gone back to sleep and was snoring softly. Lara slipped her kimono over her shoulders and tied the sash loosely around her waist, luxuriating in the feel of the soft silk against her body and the faint smell of rose oil from last night's bath.

For a moment, she stood and watched her husband of thirty years as he slept. She didn't love him anymore. But she was fond of him and she was happy with the easy familiarity of their lovemaking. But love? Well… It was enough that he still loved her, wasn't it? He had just told her so, hadn't he?

Opening the French doors, she stepped out onto the balcony and looked across the dam. Another wild orchid might bloom today, she thought…

Mother Superior's Garden Party

James comes forward to greet me, gallant as ever. He could be the Great Gatsby himself in his dinner suit, black tie and dazzling white shirt with his blond hair parted in the middle. I think I smell Californian poppy as he kisses me on the cheek.

'Roisin, darling. Come, let me get you some champagne.' James pours a glass of the best. 'Your brother Pat and your father have supplied twenty bottles,' he says as he hands me the glass. 'Did you know, Roisin, that Napoleon had the traditional champagne glass fashioned after Josephine's breast?' he says in that languid way that he has about him.

'Well, no, I didn't know that now, James. You look so handsome today in your dinner suit.'

He smiles back at me – a professional smile maybe – a newsreader's smile possibly but a smile nonetheless and how I need a smile just now.

Child Portrait

I have only ever seen you from an angle,
Never full countenance.
Driving you to school,
face side-on, shadow-caste
dimpled profile,
mouth set in that particular way
showing faith and in turn apprehension.
Behind a book, black eyebrows butterfly-like,
third eye well hidden
or sending text messages to friends,
head bent as if in supplication.
Three-quarter view,
cheekbones high, chiselled, promising manhood
You are too much to take in all at once.

Hands, never still,
overwhelm me with their possibilities.
Long fingers, might be musical,
the paediatrician said,
Might grow to five-foot-ten.
I am growing yet.
Only coincidence that the soles of your feet
are lined – like mine.
We travel without a genetic map you and I,
but maps are not needed for our journey.

Black hair softly on a white pillow,
skin – coffee-coloured – not from the sun.
Not the fruit of my womb.
Some say stolen from another orchard.
Some say better left where fallen,
not good to transplant seeds to foreign soil.
I say, horticulture aside,
better to be where full ripening is possible.

You are diamond-like;
I view you in discrete facets.
Endless with the inherited beauty of another mother.
Not my echo,
not my mirror,
not my glory
but yet my son,
still.

Our Darker Purpose

Scented tea light candles burning. Cinnamon, I think. Nice in a cake. Fruit cake. Someone called me a fruit cake. Don't like fruit. Rotten. How long have I been coming to her now? Once a week for seven years? Seven years' bad luck. How are things? Is your medication helping? Not really. Voices come and go. People always laughing at me. If only I could have been born beautiful like them, someone might have loved me. But true beauty shines from within, doesn't it?

Joe, 1971

The summer sun was high in the sky when Joe bought me the little silver ring. The traveller sat cross-legged on a red velvet cloth edged with gold embroidery, his feet cracked and dirty; his eyes were dark and deep and rimmed with black kohl. Over his grey dreadlocks, he wore a white headband and he smelled of incense and sandalwood. Brass bells, candlesticks, dark musky-smelling oils, silk saris, wooden bracelets were spread on the pavement under the wide welcome shade of the cedar tree.

'Would you like to look at the jewellery?' he said, smiling at me, displaying several gold teeth, and pointing to the little hexagonal glass cupboard. 'You'll like this one,' he said, handing me a silver ring, decorated with little carved roses.

I slipped it on my finger.

'Perfect,' he said hypnotically. 'You'll take it?'

'Yes,' I said, 'I'll take it.'

Joe was standing next to me holding a sword in a dark blue and gold scabbard and was staring down at it.

'That's for you, sir,' said the squatted man, his legs knotted one over the other.

'Okay,' said Joe unquestioningly and handed him the money.

As we started to walk away, I turned and looked back at him.

Pointing a long boney finger at me, he said, smiling broadly, 'You... you keep your promise!'

Peripheral Vision

All my life I have skirted on the periphery, always skating around the edges, existing on the border, looking on at life from a distance: a satellite existence. Did I read that somewhere? If I did, it resonated so completely within me that I have taken the statement as my own claimed it as the truth about my existence, my personal manifesto.

Looking down at my cracked heels and my unpainted toenails, I wonder if anyone will ever ask me out anywhere again. I used to despise feet like these – old duck's feet I would have called them once, in the arrogance of my youth. Old duck's feet, don't-care-any-more feet.

Notes

Homage to Eveline

Quoted from 'Ode to a Nightingale', John Keats (1819) –
Page 33: 'My heart aches, and a drowsy numbness pains/My sense, as though of hemlock had drunk'.

Letter from Virginia

Quoted from *A Room of One's Own*, Virginia Woolf (1929) –
Page 36: 'I need not hate any man; he cannot hurt me. I need not flatter any man, he has nothing to give me.'
Page 38: 'slip off your petticoats when it suits you'.
Quoted from *Orlando*, Virginia Woolf (1928)–
Page 38: 'the only resource now left us is to look out the window'.

Email to Virginia

Quoted from *A Room of One's Own*, Virginia Woolf (1929) –
Page 40: 'The nursemaid will heave coal. The shop woman will drive an engine.'
Page 42: 'A woman must have money and a room of her own if she is to write fiction.'